Theodore Fry, Company Barclay

A Brief Memoir of Francis Fry

F.S.A. of Bristol

Theodore Fry, Company Barclay

A Brief Memoir of Francis Fry
F.S.A. of Bristol

ISBN/EAN: 9783337402303

Printed in Europe, USA, Canada, Australia, Japan

Cover: Foto ©Andreas Hilbeck / pixelio.de

More available books at **www.hansebooks.com**

A Brief Memoir

OF

FRANCIS FRY, F.S.A.

OF BRISTOL

BY HIS SON

THEODORE FRY, M.P.

Not Published.

—

1887.

To my beloved Mother, who for more than half a century was the sharer with her husband in every joy and sorrow, the participator in all his interests, the helper in every-day life, a true and devoted wife, are these few pages in memory of a beloved Father affectionately dedicated.

PREFACE.

A desire having been expressed by many who knew the subject of this Memoir, that some details should be preserved of his literary labours, the following pages have been compiled. The sketch is very brief, and has been written in the midst of many engagements. It may perhaps serve the desired end, and sometimes bring to remembrance the figure of one of Bristol's well-known citizens, the last survivor of three brothers who, in various ways, were so long connected with her interests, and whose death has left a void in his own branch of study which no one else can fill.

WOODBURN, DARLINGTON,
September, 1887.

MEMOIR.

THE ancestors of the Fry family came originally from ~~Devonshire. The earliest authenticated not~~ice ~~is of Sir Richard Fry, Knight, of Yarty, who~~ ~~married as his second wife, Joan Beaufort, second~~ ~~daughter of Edmund Beaufort, first Duke of~~ ~~Somerset, and grandson of John of Gaunt.~~ His ~~son John married Agnes, daughter and heiress of~~ ~~Richard Yarty, in that county.*~~ ~~The descendants~~ ~~of various branches of the family are now found~~ ~~in Devonshire, Wiltshire, Bristol, London and~~ ~~Darlington.~~

In the early part of the 17th century another John Fry was settled at Sutton Benger, in Wiltshire. His father, Zephaniah Fry, who was born in 1658 (thirty-four years after George Fox), joined the Society of Friends, and in his youth may very likely have heard the stirring sermons of the founder of this section of the Christian Church.

* *See* "Genealogical History of the Kings of England," p. 384, London, 1707; also "The Visitations of Devonshire," p. 115, published by the Harleian Society. The present family still bear the arms of Sir R. Fry—Gules, three horses courant, argent.

Joseph Fry, born in 1728, son of the above-named John Fry of Sutton Benger, was the first member of this branch of the family who settled in Bristol. He entered the medical profession, and his affable courteous manner and sound Christian principles soon secured to him a large practice amongst the highest class of his fellow-citizens. Possessing uncommon energy and activity of mind, he was led to take a part in many scientific undertakings, actuated more by the desire to be useful to society and to advance the arts than by any hope of individual profit. This motive induced him to give Champion assistance in prosecuting the porcelain manufacture. Soon after Dr. Fry began to practice medicine he made chocolate, and then purchased the patentright of Churchman. The chocolate and cocoa manufactory was conducted as a distinct business, and has been carried on by the family to the present day. He was a partner in the firm of Fry and Pine, type-founders, of Bristol. About 1770 the business was removed to London, under the firm of Isaac Moore and Co.; it then passed to J. Fry and Co., the other members of the firm being his sons Edmund and Henry; in later times it was carried on by one of the sons,

Joseph Fry

(From a Silhouette in the possession of the late Francis Fry.)

EDMUND FRY, M.D.

(From a Silhouette in the possession of the late Francis Fry.)

Edmund Fry, M.D., who, in his turn, admitted into partnership his son Windover, under the title of Edmund Fry and Son. In 1786 specimen books of types were issued by Joseph Fry and Sons, letter-founders to the Prince of Wales. Owing to the advanced age of Dr. Fry, the concern passed into the hands of Thoroughgood and Co. in 1828. Since that period the firm has been Thoroughgood and Besley—then R. Besley and Co.—now Sir Charles Reed and Sons—a long succession of enterprising and eminent type-founders.

Many books were printed in Bristol by William Pine, with type notably from the foundry of Fry and Pine. The London firm were also printers, and four editions of the Bible issued from their press; two in large folio and two in octavo; these last were in large type for the use of the aged. The type was cut purposely for the Bibles, and probably no handsomer and better proportioned type was ever made. In 1788 the printing business was separated from the foundry, and was placed under the care of Henry Fry, in Worship Street, under the style of the Cicero Press.

Mr. Joseph Fry was also, to the time of his death, a partner with the late Alderman William

Fripp, under the firm of " Fry, Fripp and Co., soap boilers." Mr. Fry was a good chemist for his day, and much improved the quality of the manufacture, and laid the foundation of the celebrity of that soap house, which has continued to the present time, now in the hands of Christopher Thomas Brothers. He was admitted a Freeman of the City, 24th March, 1753. Besides all this, Mr. Joseph Fry had some chemical works at Battersea, in which he was assisted by one of his sons. He died the 29th March, 1787, after a few days' illness, aged 59 years. He was buried in the Friends' burial ground at the Friars. His funeral was largely attended, not only by his personal friends, but by his fellow-citizens—a proof of the great respect in which he was universally held.[*]

On the death of Joseph Fry his widow changed the name of the firm from Fry, Vaughan and Co., which it had hitherto been, to Anna Fry and Son.[†] In 1795 it was removed from Newgate Street to Union Street, where a Watts' steam engine was

[*] " Two Centuries of Ceramic Art in Bristol," p. 218, Owen, 1873 ; and " History of the Old English Letter Foundries," p. 298, T. B. Reed, 1887.

[†] Anna Fry was the daughter of Henry Portsmouth, M.D., of Basingstoke, and died in 1803.

ANNA FRY.

soon erected, which is believed to have been the first of the kind in the city. This son was Joseph Storrs Fry, who succeeded to the business. He took into partnership Mr. Henry Hunt, a member of the Society of Friends, and a gentleman of considerable business experience. During this partnership the firm was Fry and Hunt. Mr. Hunt retired in 1822, and Mr. Fry's three sons—Joseph, Francis, and Richard—were afterwards associated with him, under the style of J. S. Fry and Sons, the name which the firm has since borne.

Joseph Storrs Fry was a man of clear intellect and of a genial disposition, devoted to his family, and taking a deep interest in the welfare of his poorer neighbours. Amongst other matters, he paid some attention to the question of tolls on turnpike roads, and to the relative advantages of carriages and other vehicles with two and with four wheels, on which subject he published an essay in 1820. He also wrote an essay on the means of employing the poor, for which he was awarded a silver medal by the Board of Agriculture in 1818. He devoted much time to the study of the Holy Scriptures, and a little book which he published, with the title " The Necessity of Freedom from Sin," is an evidence of his aim to live the Christian life. After a short illness he died in 1835, in his 67th year.

His wife, whose maiden name was Ann Allen, was a lady whose Christian influence was widely felt in the circle in which she moved. She was a minister in the Society of Friends, and spent much time in visiting the homes of the poor around. In the colliery village of Kingswood, not far from Frenchay, she did much to promote the religious welfare of the inhabitants. The state of the people at that time often rendered these visits dangerous, so little had civilising influences been brought to bear upon them, and much good was effected through her instrumentality.

Their second son, Francis, was born at Westbury-on-Trym, near Bristol, on the 28th of October, 1808, but during most of his early life his father lived at the quiet little village of Frenchay, about five miles from Bristol, driving in almost daily to his engagements in the city.

There were also four sisters, neither of whom lived much beyond middle life. Possessing cultured intellects and great refinement of character, they added in no small degree to the development

JOSEPH STORRS FRY.

of literary taste in others and the happiness of the family circle. One of them was an excellent German scholar, and translated into English selections of Hymns by Luther, Melancthon and other writers.

In the latter village lived for several years of this period Michael Maurice and his family, and we cannot describe it better than by the following quotation from the memoirs of his son, the Rev. Frederick Denison Maurice* :—

"The village is small as it well can be. It lies in a beautiful country of rocky streams and park-land, hill and dale, with perhaps some of the finest timber in England within a short distance of it. A little hamlet, at that time chiefly of Quaker houses, nestled together along one side of a tiny village green, across which the houses look towards a deep ravine, faced on the opposite hill-sides by graceful woods. In the very middle of the village lies, as it were, as the epitome of its characteristics, a little Quaker graveyard, shut out from all the world on every side but that on which a narrow entrance running under the tiny meeting-room gives a bare approach to it, and seems to admit you to the very stillness of a Quaker meeting of the dead. There was at that time no Church. This little Quaker Meeting-house, Mr. Maurice's tiny Chapel, and the graveyards belonging to them, were the only spots devoted to sacred purposes within it."

At the neighbouring village of Fishponds was a large school, kept by a Friend named Joel

* "The Life of F. D. Maurice," vol. i., page 10.

Lean, an establishment quite as advanced in the instruction given as most of that period, and there Mr. Fry received his education. This was then supposed to be completed at an early age, especially in the case of young men about to enter into commercial life. He commenced his business training at Croydon, but from his twentieth year until middle life, devoted most of his time to the management of the ever-increasing business in Bristol in which he was afterwards a partner. In 1833 Mr. Fry married Matilda, only daughter of Daniel and Anne Penrose of Brittas, Co. Wicklow. After a short residence in the city he removed, in 1839, to Cotham, a wooded eminence between Bristol and Redland, which was then quite in the country. He built a house close to the old Tower, which he afterwards purchased, and it was his home for nearly fifty years. In the garden he took great pleasure, the Tower giving an added interest to it, as from its height and position it commands a magnificent view, and attracted many visitors.* His family consisted of four sons and three daughters, five of whom, with their mother, survive him.

* For the History of the Tower *see* Appendix B.

COTMAN NO. 2

In October, 1831, occurred the Bristol riots,
during which he acted as a special constable,
and which he thus describes :—" This day
Sir Charles Wetherel, Recorder of Bristol, made
his public entry into the city, as is usual for
the Judge of Assize. Owing to his great oppo-
sition to the Reform Bill, and his having said
that the people of Bristol did not wish reform in
Parliament, there was a determination on the part
of many to testify by visible and audible signs
their disapprobation of his conduct.   Thousands
of persons would have met him, but he came in
earlier than was expected, which fact being known
a great mob surrounded the Mansion House in
Queen Square, and after some time began throwing
stones.   Thus originated the riot, and before
night the parlour floor was ransacked by the mob.
On Sunday, Bristol was in a state of uncontrolled
rioting, like a city delivered up to an invading
army to be pillaged.   The civil power was quite
inactive and powerless.   About two o'clock, Bride-
well Prison was opened and burnt down by the
mob ; after this they attacked the new gaol and
fired the centre building, and let all the prisoners
out.   Lawford's Gate was served in the same way,

and many other buildings. On Monday the mob set fire to two sides of Queen's Square, the whole of which was destroyed, except two houses. My brother Richard and myself were in Bristol till half-past twelve o'clock last night, and again this morning soon after six o'clock. We went to the Square, and found the warehouse in which our cocoa was, on fire; nearly the whole of it was burnt. By daylight the mob was drunk with wine, &c., out of the Mayor's and other houses. They were quite worn out, so that a few soldiers dispersed them, and thus ended the rioting."

Mr. Fry took a great interest in the early railways in the West of England. He was a member of the board of the Bristol and Gloucester Railway, which held its first sitting on the 11th July, 1839, and consisted of the following gentlemen: Messrs. George Jones, Winwood, Morgan, Fison, F. Fry, Dibsdall, Rankin, Ricketts, Alexander and Osborne. He retained this position until the amalgamation of the Bristol and Gloucester Railway with that from Gloucester to Birmingham in 1845, and on that joint board until its union very soon afterwards with the Midland Railway Company. In the arrangements for these amalgamations he took a leading part. He was also one of the first subscribers to the Bristol and Exeter Railway, which was commenced in the year 1836. He did not join the board until 1854, but from that time he remained a director until the company was absorbed by the Great Western in 1876. When the South Devon Railway was constructed he formed one of the Board of Management, but as the late Mr. Brunel, who was the engineer, decided to try the then new atmospheric system, in which the majority of the board supported him, Mr. Fry withdrew, feeling sure it would not answer on such a length of railway, and he declined to be a party to sanctioning it. His fears proved too true, and it was very soon abandoned for the ordinary locomotive; had his view been taken a great loss to the shareholders would have been prevented. At a later date he returned to his old place in the South Devon Railway Company, and also joined the one still farther west, called the Devon and Cornwall Railway, as a representative of the Bristol and Exeter Company, which had a considerable amount of capital in them.

No public work, however, gave him more

pleasure and interest than the Bristol Water Works. The supply of the city was very deficient in days gone by, being chiefly obtained from wells, an evil which it was not very easy to remedy, owing to the great distance from any good and adequate source, and the great expense involved by this, as well as engineering difficulties. When the project was brought before the public in 1845, recognizing the boon it would be, he accepted a seat on the directorate, which he held uninterruptedly until his death, a period of upwards of forty years.

The original capital was £200,000. The Act received the Royal Assent on 16th July, 1846. Water was supplied by the Company in 1848. Mr. Fry was one of the provisional committee. The first directors (all of whom he survived) were Messrs. John Bates, William Budd, M.D., Charles Bowles Fripp, Francis Fry, Richard Fry, John Kerle Haberfield, William Hooper, Philip Jones, Robert Leonard, George Eddie Sanders, George Thomas, and Richard George Shum Tuckett. The present capital is one million.

After the death of Mr. Abbot in 1874, Mr. Fry occupied the post of Chairman. The directors had to contend with many difficulties in its early years, but they were all surmounted, and the undertaking has proved a success and a great blessing to his native city. No detail was too small to be beneath his notice: he made himself acquainted with everything, both at the large works at Chewton Mendip (where the first reservoirs were constructed) and elsewhere, as well as with the office management.

In all these important positions his practical knowledge and shrewd advice were much valued. He was remarkable for his keen insight into future contingencies. One of his colleagues remarked, "That he never knew any one who could see so far ahead or imagine so many possibilities." The danger sometimes lay in seeing too far, so as to endanger the advantages of the present. This natural tendency of mind often, however, proved of the greatest value, and not a few instances are known in which after events showed, sometimes when too late, that it would have been better had his counsel been followed. Practical instances of his foresight may be given. It was his great desire to see the establishment of a Parcel post by which parcels might be carried at uniform rates throughout the whole kingdom, "with punctuality and safety." As far back as 1852 he took pains to get this

effected. The only difference between his plan
and the present Parcel post lay in the fact that
he wished it carried out by the united action of all
the railway companies instead of by Her Majesty's
Government. He urged that the "convenient
collection and exact delivery twice a day under
one management" would develop an enormous
trade which would soon be very profitable, especially if the rate (except for very long distances)
were practically the same. He argued "that no
class of traffic is so suppressed for the want of
greater convenience and reduced charges." No
one at that time could prepay a parcel from one
part of the kingdom to another with certainty.
In London there was always a break; a sender
could not pay beyond, and in few towns was
there any receiving office nearer than the railway
station. It is remarkable that some of the fees he
suggested are the same as those now in force. The
scheme did not receive sufficient support from the
companies, but had they done so it is probable
that the profit now going to the Post Office on this
steadily increasing part of its business would have
been kept in their own hands. Mr. Fry lived to
see his views completely justified, and a far larger

business carried on than he had ever ventured to expect, though by a different agency.

In 1867 he proposed to the directors of the leading railway companies that they should unite in raising and guaranteeing a permanent stock to pay off their existing mortgages, many of which were then raised for definite periods only. He estimated that with such a strong guarantee £100,000,000 might be raised at $3\frac{1}{2}$ per cent., and as the prevailing rate of interest was then at least $4\frac{1}{2}$ per cent., a million a year might be saved to the companies interested; and that if this sum were allowed to accumulate for ten years it would form a reserve fund equal to every emergency possible. This stock would, he believed, soon be made a legal investment for trustees. The floating mortgages of nineteen railways at the period named were over £77,000,000, and the total net revenues were four times the amount required to pay the interest on this sum, so that there is little doubt the scheme was a safe and practicable one. The details were carefully considered, and had it received the support which it deserved would have been a great saving to the ordinary shareholders.

Mr. Fry had a keen appreciation of the beautiful,

whether in nature or in art, but the bent of his mind was in the direction of antiquarian pursuits. He was ably assisted by his wife, whose tastes were akin to his own, and whose wide reading and accurate knowledge enabled her to render him, during more than half a century, invaluable help, which he always loved to acknowledge.

Before railways had made their appearance, and when travelling was accomplished only by the old diligence or by private carriage, they took, in company with some intimate friends, two long journeys on the continent; in 1852 they went to Germany, and in 1857 visited, with some members of their family, Northern Italy and Rome. This latter tour, which included a drive along the Riviera from Marseilles to Genoa, was replete with interest and rich in memories of classic and mediæval times. During these journeys several of the capitals of Europe were visited, their art galleries and museums proving always the chief objects of attraction.

Mr. Fry had visited Northern Italy before in 1850. About that time the Society of Friends had arranged to send deputations with a memorial to every crowned Head in Europe, praying for the abolition of slavery in their respective dominions; or if they were free in this respect, to ask them to use their influence with other States.

These visits were first suggested under a strong sense of religious duty by William Forster (father of the late Right Hon. W. E. Forster, M.P.), who afterwards died in Tenessee, U.S.A., when on a visit to that country in connection with the same movement.

Mr. Forster himself volunteered for the service on every occasion, and for three months in the above year was accompanied by Mr. Fry and the late Mr. Robert Alsop, of London. This was a time of peculiar interest. The object of their visit and the letters of introduction they carried from the Foreign Office, obtained them interviews seldom accorded to such visitors. They were received by Cabinet Ministers and persons in high stations in many of the States (being before the days of Italian unity). They saw, amongst others, King Victor Emanuel and Count Cavour in Turin, the Grand Duke of Tuscany at Florence, and the Grand Dukes of Parma and Modena. In Milan, Verona, Venice, Pisa, Genoa, and other large towns, they paid calls on all persons of influence, and were invariably, both in political and religious circles, most courteously received. Amongst other names may be mentioned the Duke of Bordeaux, grandson of Charles X., Marshal Marmont, Duke de Ragusa, the Patriarch of Venice, and Marshal Radetzky, Commander of the Austrian Army of Occupation, then in his 84th year. The Address was also circulated in French and German. The letter accompanying it was as follows :—

" L'Indirizzo qui annesso della Società Religiosa degli Amici della Gran Bretagna e l'Irlanda ai Sovrani ed a coloro che sono investiti di Autorità tra i popoli che fanno professione di essere cristiani, ha per iscopo di chiamar l'attenzione di tutti gli Amici dell'umanità *sulla crudeltà e l'ingiustizia della Tratta dei neri e sulla iniquità della schiavitù dei neri.* E'caldamente raccomandato alla lettura seria ed all'esame coscienzioso delle persone che hanno veramente a cuore il benessere del loro prossimo.

" WILLIAM FORSTER.*

" FRANCIS FRY.

" ROBERT ALSOP.

" Genova, 17th 5th mo., 1850."

The time thus spent afforded many opportunities for acquiring knowledge, and assisted largely in the culture of his natural taste. The art galleries and museums in Florence, Bologna, Venice, and many

---

* *See* "Memoirs of William Forster" (Bennett, 1865). Vol. II., page 284.

other places, gave him the greatest delight. The
beautiful forms of the Greek or Etruscan vases
and other vessels charmed his eye. His own
house, in many ways so simple and unostentatious,
testified to his appreciation of their exquisite
workmanship.

The study of coins afforded him great interest.
The historical knowledge which it strengthened
was one of its greatest charms, and in many
journeys an interested lookout was kept for
souvenirs of bygone days. His love of natural
science was also great, although the opportunities
of acquiring systematic knowledge were very
different from those of the present day. As a
young man, he formed a collection of minerals
and fossils from the chalk formations; and at a
later period, recent shells occupied his attention,
especially those minute forms gathered in deep-
sea dredgings on our own coast.

Mr. Fry was a member of the Managing Committee of the Bristol Philosophical Society for
many years, as well as of the large subscription
Library which existed long before the Free
Libraries Act came into operation. In the former
he met the most scientific men of the city. The

geologists, George Stuchbury and Robert Etheridge (now head of the Geological Department at South Kensington), were curators at the Bristol Museum during the greater part of this period, and added largely to its collections. Scientific men like Dr. Pritchard and Dr. Estlin, of Bristol, it was always a pleasure to him to meet, and lecturers from a distance he was ever ready to welcome. He thus became acquainted with James Silk Buckingham, Dr. Wolff (both celebrated travellers), and with many other men of note in their day who have now all passed away. In the Museum, which is one of the best in the provinces, Mr. Fry felt some natural pride, especially in its collection of minerals. It is rich in Palæontological remains; the Ichthyosaura and Plethiosaura from the coal formations form a splendid series, and he was never weary of explaining them to his family or to visitors.

Mr. Fry's name will, however, be more associated with books and china than with anything else. His collection of the latter consisted principally (though by no means exclusively) of specimens produced at the Bristol factory between the years 1768-1781. His grandfather, as before mentioned, was a shareholder in these works, and some of the well-known "Bristol Jars" have never been out of the possession of the family.* Some of the pieces have special interest, as, for instance, the richly-ornamented cup and saucer which formed a part of the service presented by R. and J. Champion† as a token of friendship to Mrs. Edmund Burke, "the best of British wives," on the 3rd November, 1774, after her husband's successful contest in Bristol. Part of this service was in the possession of the late Mr. W. R. Callender of Manchester. Mr. Burke, on the same occasion, presented to Mrs. Smith, the wife of a merchant with whom he resided when in Bristol, a beautiful tea service, with her initials "S. S." on the pieces, as a souvenir of their kindness to him. Specimens of this interesting set are also included in the Fry Cabinet.

He was always fond of books, but collected

---

* Those who are interested in this subject will find in Mr. Owen's most valuable work, "Two Centuries of Ceramic Art in Bristol, 1873," a full description, with wood-cuts, of many pieces in this collection, including the vases. Mr. Fry gave much assistance to Mr. Owen in the production of this work, which he therein gratefully acknowledges.

† The manufacturer and his wife.

chiefly with reference to special objects. At one time he endeavoured to procure all the literature of the 17th and 18th centuries which in any way illustrated the history of the Society of Friends. The works and lives of its early members— showing their sufferings for conscience sake, and the way in which a firm allegiance to the simple commands of Christ in reference to oaths and other points led, in the end, to religious liberty and privileges which, until recently, no other sect enjoyed—were of the deepest interest to him. Their adherence to peace principles during the Irish Rebellion of 1792, and on other occasions, and their wonderful preservation and escapes when in great danger, because of their refusal to bear arms either as soldiers or for personal defence, can be clearly seen in some of these works. This collection, which, though not of interest to the general reader in the present day, is very complete—almost unique of its kind, and which could scarcely be gathered together again—may yet be of service to any who want to refer to the various phases of religious thought and controversial questions which they illustrate.

The productions of the early printing presses,

the "Incunabula," as they were called up to the year 1500, were also greatly valued by Mr. Fry. In the year 1860 he spent three months in Germany with his wife and two members of his family, the writer of these pages being one of them. They visited many places connected with the early history of printing—Worms, Mayence, Spires, Stuttgard, &c., &c. At Mayence, its birth-place, they saw the old cellar in which Gutenberg* worked, and the original cross-bar of the first press, marked "J. MCDXLI. G." Of the owner of this most interesting relic he purchased a beautiful early printed book, which King Ludwig I. of Bavaria had sent from the library at Munich in remembrance of his visit to the same house. Worms, the birth-place of the first English New Testament (to which reference will be made later on), was especially interesting to him.

Several weeks were spent at Münich, and many hours were passed in the magnificent Library in that city, where every facility was granted him by the authorities; and here he unexpectedly discovered the books printed at Worms by Peter Schœffer, the younger, which enabled him to decide that the

* See Appendix A.

first Tyndale's Testament was from Schœffer's Press at Worms. The two works identical in every respect with it were "Alle Propheten" and a "Treatise on Bergwerck" (Mining), both in German.

Mr. Fry's general library was small. He was not a book buyer as many are. He bought with an object: books about books, such as the early history of printing, on writing, engraving, and on bibliography in general. Dibdin's celebrated works were great favourites, and of these he had a complete series. In the purchase of MSS. he did not indulge to any extent, but a few Horæ or Missals he appreciated on account of their exquisite penmanship and illuminations. His name is more known in connection with the English Bible than anything else, not as a collector only, but by the works he published. There have been many valuable collections made before, such as Lea Wilson's, George Offer's, and others; but probably no one endeavoured to make his studies so subservient to a systematic and historical account of the various editions of the different translators. The subject first attracted his attention about the year 1850, so that his knowledge was the growth of five and thirty years; and having once taken it up he brought to bear upon it untiring industry, great patience, practical business ability, and a most retentive memory. He never forgot any book which he had once seen or heard of, and could always remember imperfections in any of his collection without reference. At first it was only in leisure hours or after the engagements of the day that he began to study his Bibles and Testaments. As years rolled by, and business cares devolved on others, it became almost a life work, and that of the deepest interest. As his name became known, books were sent to him from all parts of the country, and these were often collated to see how far they were perfect.

The object which Mr. Fry had first in view was to obtain information about all the various issues which had been printed to the date of the Authorized Version of 1611. The interest extending, he did not stop at that year but continued to add copies from various presses, even up to the New Version of 1881-5. He devoted much attention to the editions of the translations by William Tyndale, Miles Coverdale, and Archbishop Cranmer; and with this object he was in constant correspondence with a large number of persons who possessed copies of any of them, sparing no trouble in personally visiting public or private Libraries where treasured volumes could be inspected or compared. He always received the greatest kindness from the fortunate possessors of rare copies, and the Quaker gentleman in the old costume, now almost obsolete, had the fullest access granted him to the Royal Library at Windsor, to that at Lambeth Palace, to the magnificent collection of Earl Spencer at Althorpe, to that of the late Earl of Ashburnham at Ashburnham Place, the Earl of Leicester's at Holkham Hall, the Marquis of Northampton's at Castle Ashby, the Earl of Pembroke's at Wilton, Lord Zouche's at Parham, and many others.

At the Library of the British Museum he was a constant visitor, being well-known to Mr. George Bullen, the head of that department, as well as to his predecessors, the late Mr. Winter Jones and Mr. Panizzi. At the Bodleian at Oxford, Dr. Bandinell, and subsequently Mr. Cox, offered him all the assistance in their power, and his information was often of great use to them. Not a few foreign libraries were laid under contribution by him, especially when endeavouring to trace the birthplace of the earliest editions, as he had often to seek other books printed with the same type and on paper with the same water-mark, to show the origin of some testament printed without date or printer's name. Of water-marks he had a considerable variety.

Amongst private collectors he had a large acquaintance, and it was one of his greatest delights to meet with men of similar taste and compare notes with them, or to be able to assist others who needed information, which few were so able to impart as himself upon critical questions of precedence or variation in texts or words. He was thus brought into connection with collectors like the late Henry Stevens (who assisted him in many ways), Henry Bohn, Samuel Addington, and Henry Huth; with students like Dr. Gotch of the Baptist College, Bristol, Dr. Gott, then Vicar of Leeds, the late Dr. Hook, Dean of Chichester, Dr. Burgon, the present Dean, Lord Arthur Hervey, now Bishop of Bath and Wells, the late Dr. Baylee of St. Aidans, Liverpool, the late William Ewing of Glasgow, the late Archdeacon Cotton of Thurles, the late Rev. Robert

Daly, Bishop of Cashel, the Rev. Nicholas Pocock of Bristol, the late Rev. R. Demaus, Edward Arber, F.S.A., London, and many other well-known names. With the late James Lenox, of New York, the founder of the great Library which he bequeathed to that city, and with the late George Livermore of Philadelphia, Mr. Fry had epistolary intercourse which resulted in practical benefit to the collection of Bibles in New York. These friendships brought a large correspondence, besides which it was no light work to keep a constant look out for copies, in book-sellers' catalogues or in auction sales, and to answer enquiries from those who were constantly writing to ask him the value of any old Bibles in their possession; many hoping (like the owner of a Queen Anne farthing) that his imperfect "Gene-van," or his well-thumbed copy of a "Breeches Bible," might prove, if not a Coverdale, at least of great money value to its fortunate possessor.

In the year 1864 he was much gratified in receiv-ing from the Emperor Alexander II. of Russia a copy of the facsimile of the "Codex Sinaiticus," which had just been published by Royal command by Dr. Tischendorf of Leipsic. It was one of the first sent to this country, and was subsequently enriched by an autograph of the Imperial donor and a letter from the Russian Ambassador in London, Baron Korf, couched in the politest terms. This wonderful work in four folio volumes was one of 325 (to which the edition was limited), and the cost of which was £30,000. One hundred were given to Dr. Tischendorf to sell, the rest were presented by the Emperor to public or private libraries.

The discovery of this ancient Codex at the Monastery of St. Catherine on Mount Sinai in 1859 attracted great attention at the time, and the discoverer offered to place some of his MSS. in the hands of Mr. Fry, if they would be of any use to him in his biblical researches. The Czar graciously accepted copies of Mr. Fry's works for the Imperial Library.

It was only natural that with the work of the British and Foreign Bible Society, Mr. Fry would take a deep interest. The small but choice collection of early specimens in its library he knew well and assisted to perfect. Many of the "deputations" to the annual meetings at Bristol spent pleasant hours amongst the old books, and have testified to the help which they obtained from him on some question of interest, and to the encouragement derived from a closer acquaintance with the "ancestors of the volume without note or comment" which they sought so diligently to circulate. The differences which exist in some passages were well-known and carefully pointed out to the visitor. The text of William Tyndale, which in some places sounds quaint and old-fashioned, he much liked; and a return to it in sundry places in the Revised Version was hailed by him with much satisfaction, as in John x. 16, the word "fold" is superseded by "flock," which gives a much more comprehensive meaning to the text. On the whole, he much preferred the Authorised Version. His love for William Tyndale amounted almost to veneration. He considered him, and rightly so, as one of the greatest men England ever produced. In order to make his text more generally known, and to stimulate interest in the great translator, Mr. Fry determined to give to the public an exact facsimile* of the only known perfect copy of Tyndale's Testament (1525-6) in existence, if indeed it can be called

* *See* Appendix C.

perfect without a title page. It belongs to the Library of the Baptist College in Bristol, having been bequeathed to it with other books in 1784 by Dr. Andrew Gifford, who purchased it for twenty guineas of Mr. John White, who in his turn obtained it at Mr. Langford's sale of Mr. Ames' books on May 13th, 1760. Mr. Ames, it seems, gave fifteen shillings for it. Before this it had been in the possession of Lord Oxford, who was so delighted with obtaining it that he settled £20 a year on Mr. John Murray, who procured it for him.* The pleasure felt by Mr. Ames at obtaining this volume is shown in the following letter, addressed to Mr. George Ballard :—

"Wapping, June 30, 1748.

" I cannot forbear telling you of my good success in buying at Lord Oxford's sale the phœnix of the whole library: I mean the first English Testament that ever was printed in the year 1526. It has been thought no perfect one was left from the flames. My lord was so well, pleased in being the possessor of it, that he gave the person (Mr. John Murray) he had it of, ten guineas, and settled an annuity of twenty pounds a year during the person's life, which is yet paid to him. The particulars are too many to commit to a letter ; the old historians and Fox give a good account of it." †

* There is an imperfect copy in the Library of St. Paul's Cathedral.

† "Cotton Editions of the Bible in English," 2nd edition, 1852, page 2.

The book was not in its original cover,* and had Mr. Ames' name stamped on both sides; it is 5¾ by 4 inches in size, and had evidently been in the possession of some person of note, as all the wood-cuts, capitals, and paragraph marks, 2606 in number, were illuminated. It is not known if ever there was a title; and if so, it probably did not bear the translator's name, as he says in another place, "The cause why I set my name before this little treatise, and have not rather done it in the New Testament is, that when I folowed the councel of Chryste, which exhorteth men (Math. vi.) to do their good deades secretly, and to be contente with the conscience of wel doynge, and that God seeth us, and paeyentlye to abyde the rewarde of the last day which Chryste hath purchased for us; and nowe wold faine have done lykewise, but am compelled otherwise to do."†

This reproduction of perhaps the most interesting book in our language was an exact facsimile, taken on tracing paper and lithographed in the usual way. To prove the correctness of the work, Mr. Fry personally compared a proof copy with

* Mr. Fry's Introduction, p. 12.
† Preface to "The Wicked Mammon," ed. 1549.

Facsimile of Page of
Tyndale's New Testament, 1525.

The Epistle off the
Apostle Paul / to the Ro/
maynes.

The fyrst Chapter.

Paul the servaunte off Jesus Christ / called vnto the office off an apostle / putt a parte to preache the gospell of God / which he promysed afore by his prophetts / i the holy scriptures that make mession of his sone / the which was begotten of the seede of David / as pertaynynge to the flesshe: and declared to be the sonne of God with power of the holy goost / that sanctifieth / sence the tyme that Jesus Christ oure lorde rose agayne from deeth / by whom we have receaved grace and apostleshippe / that att all gentiles shulde obeye to the fayth which is in his name / of the which noumbre are ye also / which are Jesus Christes by vocacion.

To all you of Rome beloved of God / ād sanctes by callynge. Grace be with you and peace from God oure father / and from the lorde Jesus Christ.

Fyrst verely I thanke my god thorow Jesus Christ for you all / because youre faith is publisshed through out all the worlde. For god is my

A a

the original, line by line, and it may be depended
upon as being exact. The paper was made expressly for the purpose, to imitate that in the
original, and the same wire marks appear as in
that used by Tyndale's printer. Great pains were
taken to ascertain who this was, and where he
lived; and there is every probability that Mr. Fry
has settled this point. It was well known that
Tyndale "went over the sea," as he found "no
roume in my lorde of London's palace to trans-
late the New Testamente; but also that there was
no place to do it in all Englande, as experience
doth now openly declare." The translator went
to Hamburg, Cologne, and Worms, at which latter
place the first New Testament in English saw the
light in 1525-6. Mr. Fry proved that the printer
was Peter Schoeffer, the second son of the great
Peter Schoeffer of Mayence, partner with John
Faust. Peter Schoeffer, jun., became a Lutheran,
and settled in Worms, where he printed a Pro-
testant Bible in German, and other works, and
was denounced as a printer of heretical books. In
the libraries of Stuttgard and Munich, books from
this press were found printed, of the same size,
from the same type, with similar woodcuts and

capital letters, and the water-mark of the same design as in the New Testament. This investigation occupied no small amount of time and patience, but anything which tended to throw light on the work of this great Martyr was always a labour of love.

The following are selected from many letters referring to this work :—

From the late J. Lenox, Esq., New York.

29th March, 1866.

My Dear Sir,

   . . . A few hours' leisure and a rainy day have enabled me to look over your book, and I congratulate you upon what you have effected. It is a labour which they only who have tried the work can properly appreciate. It is not only a wonderful, but a superb volume, especially the copy upon vellum, for which I thank you especially.

I remain, Dear Sir,

Yours very truly,

J. LENOX.

From Edward Peacock, Esq., Botherford Manor, Brigg.

15th January, 1865.

You have done a good work by reproducing Tyndale's New Testament, such as will make men grateful to you wherever and as long as our language is spoken. How very faithful, on the whole, Tyndale's translation is. How much superior, indeed, is his nervous English to what we should have at the present time if the work had to be done now.

No one can appreciate Tyndale and the Authorised Version as they deserve who has not read some of the modern attempts at translation.

Believe me, my dear Sir,

Yours very truly,

EDWARD PEACOCK.

One other work may be mentioned here in connection with the Tyndale translation, though it was the last he published (1878). This was no less than a most careful and critical description of all the New Testaments of Tyndale's Version known to be in existence—forty in number. Nos. 1, 2 and 3 were published before his martyrdom. There are very few which are exactly like the others; some differ considerably from any other edition. Nos. 39 and 40 are only known to exist in the Lenox Library, New York; and the illustrations of these were obtained by photographs. Two others are also described in order to prove that they were not the Tyndale Version, as generally supposed, but the Bishop's.

Of these forty Testaments, Mr. Fry had twenty-eight in his own library. A year before his death, a title-page of a Tyndale Testament was sent to him for inspection, and was dated 1532. No copy printed in this year is known to exist, and it is different from all others. As the title-page only has been found, nothing can be said about the book. It is possibly a proof of some design for a Testament which was not printed till a later date, and with another title-page. The whole edition may have been destroyed.*

The plan pursued by the author was to examine certain thirteen chapters and 475 other verses in every edition, and note the smallest differences. These are given in exact facsimile on seventy-three plates, demy quarto, and include forty title-pages and eighty-one whole pages, &c. There are 220 pages of letter-press in the work.

The Testament printed in 1535 possesses a different orthography from any of the others. It has no printer's name or residence, and no light has ever been thrown upon the cause of this, though Mr. Fry published a long list of the words, and an inquiry soliciting information. The letter " e " is introduced wherever possible, as " aboede " for abode, " aloene " for alone, " doeth " for doth, "maede" for made, &c. It may have been through the person who wrote it out or composed the

*It is in the possession of the Rev. Dr. Angus, Regent's Park. A facsimile page of this Testament is given in Appendix D.

type being a foreigner, or that the Bible was intended to be more in accordance with some provincial dialect. A Preface gives interesting information about Tyndale, a photograph of the likeness at Hertford College, Oxford, and a fac-simile of the only autograph letter of Tyndale's known to exist. In reference to this ·Work, the late Rev. Thomas Lathbury of Bristol wrote before it was published :—

" The book, I see more and more, will be most important. It will be *unique*. No other man could have done it. Every man has some one thing which he can do better than anybody else; I allude to literary matters. I shall look upon this work of yours as one of the most important contributions to the cause of sacred bibliography. You are doing with Bibles what I have in some respects done with Prayer Books." ·

The following letters allude to the same book:—

From John Hirst, Esq., Ladcastle, Dobcross, Saddleworth.

31st May, 1880.

My Dear Sir,

. . . . I have, and highly value, your book on Tyndale's New Testament. On reading it I was greatly pleased with your treatment of the Martyr, William Tyndale. We scarcely know how much we in England are indebted to Tyndale; perhaps it would only be an understatement if we said that he did more for real civil and religious liberty than any one else. I wish you would do for his Pentateuch as you have so nobly done for his Testament, and I am sorry I can give no assistance; but pray do what you can, as no living man knows so much about him as you evidently do.

I am, yours faithfully,

JOHN HIRST.

To Francis Fry, Esq., F.S.A.

From the Rev. Aubrey Townshend, Woodbine Farm, Hewish, Bristol.

23rd September, 1880.

Dear Friend,

I am much gratified by your exceeding kindness, and shall ever value your beautiful book as a gift, not only for its very unusual worth, but for its donor's sake, and as a memento of days which I cannot easily forget—that have been fraught with singular happiness to myself—which have been spent in your society among the wonderful Bibles which are the sacred remains of the Reformation time.

Believe me ever

Your affectionately obliged,

AUBREY TOWNSHEND.

Before quite passing away from the name of Tyndale, it should be mentioned that in the erection of the monument to his memory on Nibley Knoll, Gloucestershire, in November, 1866, as well as in that of the statue on the Embankment in 1885, Mr. Fry took a warm interest, especially in the former, which was in the native county of the Reformer.

The work published in 1865, describing the

" Great Bible " and the six editions of Cranmer's translation (with two variations), and the Authorised Version of 1611, occupied many years. It is a monument of untiring industry, and an evidence of the care which the author bestowed to make his descriptions accurate and reliable. It is a folio volume, and was dedicated (by permission) to the late Right Hon. the Earl of Ashburnham, who took great interest in its progress. In the limits of this sketch it is almost impossible to give any idea of the labour it involved.

The Great Bible was printed under the auspices of Thomas Cromwell, Earl of Essex, in 1539. It was followed very closely by six editions of Archbishop Cranmer's in 1540 and 1541 : all the same size, with titles and other matter much the same, but with an introduction or prologue of his own, which ought not to be found in the Great Bible. It is believed that twenty-one thousand copies were printed in these three years, one being placed in every church by order of King Henry VIII. In the binding of these various editions, leaves became intermixed. It was also found that copies bearing the same date differed from each other in various parts. Care had to be taken in these examinations only to notice leaves which had evidently formed part of the original volumes. Perfect copies of these noble folios without inter-mixture are extremely rare.

The result of much patient investigation con-vinced Mr. Fry that portions of different editions were made use of to make one volume, when they were severally first made up. This could be done, because five editions have sixty-five lines on a page, and read together. Two others (and the same two with reprints) have sixty-two lines on a page. The great difficulty lay in obtaining a standard of authority on which he could rely. There is no whole set of the nine books known except in the British Museum and in his own collection. He soon found that the former had .incorrect leaves in them ; he therefore resolved to collate as many of these Bibles as he could find elsewhere, and did most carefully examine no fewer than 146 copies from different parts of the United Kingdom. Only thirty-one were found correct, and 115 more or less intermixed. This comparison could only be made by placing copies side by side. As many as forty lay open on a table at one time, of which some were lent.

Other copies he had to see in the libraries of their owners, taking some of his own for the sake of comparison. He proved that every leaf of each of the seven editions was different, with fourteen exceptions, where a leaf or two was common to two editions. So minute was the examination, that he observed all such differences in spelling as the following in the word "saying" in Matthew x., second column, line 38 :—"sayige," "sayinge," "saying," "sayenge," "sayig."

The set in the Fry collection may be now considered as the "standard of weight and measure" of these Cranmer Bibles, such as exists nowhere else; the nearest approach to them is in the Lenox Library, New York. Both savants had launched upon the same voyage of discovery unknown to each other at first; their introduction by the late Mr. Henry Stevens proved to their subsequent mutual advantage. There is no evidence to show that Archbishop Cranmer had anything to do with the Great Bible of Cromwell; but as it is the same size as his editions, and published nearly at the same time, it has been called by Cranmer's name. In the same volume are described the first five folio editions of the Authorised Version, which were treated in the same way. There were two issues printed in 1611, and one each in 1613, 1617, 1634, and 1640. These ponderous volumes were examined in the same manner as the Cranmers, and with equal care. The result proved that there had been great intermixture at the time of binding. The two issues of 1611, though very nearly identical, differ sufficiently to show that there were two, and that one was published before the other.* A complete and perfect set of these six Bibles is also in the library at Tower House, Bristol.

In the work now referred to will be found all the information which was gathered during years of patient labour. Reference to it will enable the owner of any leaf of a Cranmer Bible or an Authorized Version to ascertain to which edition it belongs. There are thirty-three plates of facsimile, shewing the variations in certain places in the Cranmer and eighteen of the Authorized Version, besides two sets of tables shewing the result of his comparisons. An original leaf is bound up of all the various books described, which greatly adds to the interest of the volume.

* *See* " Description of Great Bible, &c.," pp. 21-28.

The following selected letters will shew how this work was appreciated by those who were well able to judge of its merits :—

From the Right Hon. the (late) Earl of Ashburnham.

Dear Sir,

Your obliging letter reached me yesterday, and to-day I have received the two copies of your work on the early English Bibles. In point of beauty and as specimens of typography they greatly exceed my expectations; and I may feel very proud of having such a volume dedicated to me, however conscious I may be that I hardly deserve such an honour. I will very gladly add to them the facsimile of the Cambridge copy on vellum of the edition of 1539.

Believe me to be,

Very sincerely yours,

(Signed)   ASHBURNHAM.

Ashburnham Place, November 28, 1865.

From the (late) Earl of Crawford and Balcarres (then Lord Lindsay.)

My Dear Sir,

On arriving here a few days ago, I found your very kind present of a volume which is a *chef d'œuvre* in its kind— a miracle of labour, the result of love. I have read the introduction with great interest, and nothing can be more clear and satisfactory than the data for verification supplied by the plates, as well as the other illustration matter. Your idea of adding original leaves of the different Bibles will facilitate comparison in a manner that nothing else could equal. I cordially congratulate you on having achieved a work which must always hold a place of high honour in the library of bibliography, and which to the collector or amateur of old English Bibles or old English literature is invaluable. . . .

Yours very sincerely,
(Signed)   LINDSAY.

Haigh, 3rd January, 1866.

From J. H. Bohn, Esq., 13, Wellington Street, W.C.

Dear Sir,

    I am exceedingly obliged by your very kind offer of your truly invaluable work on the Bibles, and shall have the greatest pleasure in referring to it as often as I can. I have on various occasions had to borrow a copy, and can confidently assert that for accuracy it is a most wonderful performance.

I have the honour to be,
Your obliged and obedient Servant,
JOHN H. BOHN.

Francis Fry, Esq.

From Edward Arber, Esq., F.S.A., Southgate, London.

26th March, 1878.

My Dear Mr. Fry,

    . . . I have been exceedingly pleased with the book which your son was good enough to lend me—your folio on the Cranmer Editions. I had no previous knowledge of it. It is another splendid piece of work. Really you can rest from your labours, and your works will remain to all time. Thanking you again for your repeated kindnesses, and praying God always to bless you,

I am, my dear Mr. Fry,
Ever faithfully yours,
EDWARD ARBER.

F. Fry, Esq., Cotham House, Bristol.

In 1867 Mr. Fry published a Treatise on the
First English Bible, translated by Myles Coverdale
in 1535, which was dedicated to King Henry VIII.
and his "dearest and just wyfe and most vertuous
Pryncesse Quene Anne." The book is of the
greatest rarity. It seems very doubtful if more
than one copy is in existence precisely as it left
the printer's hands (except the map). It is in the
library of the Marquis of Northampton at Castle
Ashby.* The date on the title-page is 1535.
There are title-pages in the copies of the Earl of
Leicester at Holkham Hall and in the British
Museum dated 1535, but they are not exactly the
same as the one named above. There are two
titles in existence the same as the last-mentioned,
only dated 1536, one of which was in the possession
of the Countess of Jersey, Osterley Park, Middlesex;
the other is in the Library of Gloucester Cathedral.
Those interested in the history of this book are
referred to Mr. Fry's account of the same. No
light has yet been thrown upon the printer
employed by Coverdale, nor the place where it was
printed; but the result of long investigation led
him to the conclusion that it was neither at

* "Fry on Coverdale," p. 23.

Frankfort nor at Zurich, as generally supposed, but that the honour very probably belongs to Van Meteren of Antwerp. The following letter refers to this volume :—

From the late Rev. J. C. Robertson, Precincts, Canterbury.

October 15, 1872.

My Dear Mr. Fry,

Through some unaccountable carelessness I omitted, while writing to you this morning, to say anything about your book on Coverdale's Bible. Allow me now to beg pardon for the omission, and to thank you for the book, both in my own name and in that of our Chapter. The amount of care, labour, knowledge and skill which you have brought to bear on the subject of the book is quite wonderful.

Believe me, very truly yours,

J. C. ROBERTSON.

The only other books published by Mr. Fry were reprints, and as they are described in the list at the close of this volume, little need be said about them here. Two of the originals are unique —" The Prophete Jonas," by William Tyndale, and " The Proper Dyaloge," in reference to which we quote from the *Athenæum*, November 21, 1863 :— " In the same volume of tracts that contained ' The Prophete Jonas ' there was found another small work, likewise of the Reformation period, and unique, which Mr. Fry (with the permission

of Lord Arthur Hervey) has also published in facsimile, with an introduction. This is ‘ The Proper
Dyaloge betwene a Gentillman and a Husbandman,’ &c. Both of these works are remarkably
curious and interesting, not only in a bibliographical point of view, but in a literary and
historic sense as well; so that Mr. Fry has done
good service in reproducing them.”

In reference to one other reprint, we quote
from *The London Review*, April 15, 1865 :—“ Mr.
Fry not long ago issued a facsimile of ‘ The
Christian Soldiers’ Pocket Bible, showing from the
Holy Scriptures the soldier’s duty and encouragement,’ a small manual prepared for use in
Cromwell’s army, and believed to have been very
generally read by the soldiers of the Roundhead
party. A copy of this facsimile having found
its way to America, it has been reprinted, and it is
stated that some hundreds of thousands have been
distributed among the Federal soldiers there, at
the cost of one or two earnest individuals who
desired to inspire the men with the feelings of
those Ironsides who were equally good at praying
and fighting. Although a great number, in all
probability, were distributed in Cromwell’s time,

only one original is at this moment preserved to us, and that copy is in the British Museum.

We have now referred to all the works which bear Mr. Fry's name. Some of them are of more value to the collector than to any one else, but they will always be standard authorities upon the various versions they describe. No one before him so critically examined them, or recorded with such exactness the result of his labours. No one in the future, it may be safely said, will have the same opportunities which he had, or the same taste for careful comparison. Any one requiring information will rather make use of that which will lie ready to hand through the labours we have thus very briefly attempted to describe.

No attempt has been made to enter into Mr. Fry's private life. He took a deep interest in many of the great social questions of the day. When a young man he was one of four who founded the earliest temperance society in Bristol, which was then only an association to discourage the use of ardent spirits, but which led up to a much greater question. The British and Foreign Bible Society received his support and interest

long before he turned his attention to the history
of the English Bible as a distinct branch of bibliography. The Anti-slavery Society, which agitated
the public mind for many years of his life, and in
which the Society of Friends took so prominent a
part, found in him an earnest advocate. He was
a true Christian, a devoted husband (for over fifty-
three years), a kind and wise father, a firm friend,
and a helper of many in time of need. He was
warmly attached to the principles of the Society of
Friends, in which he had been educated. His
personal wants were of a simple character; he was
self-denying and anxious to promote the happiness
of others. Home and family were his great attrac-
tions after business hours. He did not accept
positions of a public character, except as mentioned; he was often solicited to join the City
Council, but he did not feel he had time enough to
spare to warrant his doing so. It has been shown
that his chief pleasure, when he could take a holi-
day, was found in travelling. The Bible which he
loved was not merely viewed by him with an
antiquarian eye; it was his daily companion from
early life in a far higher sense. His belief in it
as the revealed will and love of God to man in

Christ Jesus was bright and strong. He lived and died in the faith and hope of the Gospel, and in perfect trust in the atoning sacrifice of his Lord and Saviour Jesus Christ. His death took place on the 12th of November 1886, soon after the completion of his 83rd year. He was buried in the Friends' grave-yard at King's Weston, near Bristol.

APPENDIX A.

THE following letters, &c., will be read with interest, and are published with the permission of the writers.

Extract from the proceedings of the Directors of the Bristol Waterworks Company, at their Board Meeting held on Saturday, 20th November, 1886.

Resolved unanimously, that the Directors of the Bristol Waterworks Company desire to record their sincere regret at the great loss which the Company and they themselves have sustained by the death of their esteemed colleague and Chairman, Francis Fry, Esquire, a member of their board from the commencement of the Company, upwards of forty years since, and one who was always ready to devote his time and exceptional ability to the interests of the proprietors, and whose considerate and kindly disposition won him the loyal and affectionate regard of every person connected with the Company.

The Directors, in offering, on behalf of the Company, to Mrs. Fry and the members of the family this tribute to the memory of their late friend, wish to assure them of their deep and heartfelt sympathy.

(Signed)   ALFRED J. ALEXANDER,
Secretary and General Manager.

Resolution passed by Bristol Wagon Works Company, Limited, 22nd November, 1886.

The Directors desire to express to Mrs. Fry and the family of the late Mr. Francis Fry their heartfelt sympathy with them in the great loss they have sustained by his death ; and they take this opportunity of placing on record their high sense of his worth, and of the loss which they themselves experience by his death, associated as he has been with the Company from its first formation.

From the British and Foreign Bible Society.

146, Queen Victoria Street, E.C.,
22nd November, 1886.

Mrs. Francis Fry, Cotham, Bristol.

My dear Mrs. Fry,

At the last meeting of the Committee, Mr. J. B. Braithwaite communicated the intelligence of the death of Mr. Francis Fry. It was received by the Committee with deep regret, and I was instructed to convey to you the assurance of the high regard in which they hold the memory of your late husband, and also to express their sincere sympathy with you and your family in your painful bereavement. We are probably more indebted to the late Mr. Fry than to any other man for our increased knowledge of the history of the various versions of the English Bible—a service which the Committee of this Society are able fully to appreciate. They are at the same time happy to know that his literary interest in the sacred Scriptures sprang from his conviction of their Divine origin, and his personal faith in the Saviour whom they reveal.

Believe me, with Christian regards, to remain, dear Mrs. Fry,

Yours very faithfully,
(Signed) Wm. Major Paull,
Secretary.

From John Angus, Esq., Kirkcudbright.

16th November, 1886.

Dear Miss Fry,

. . . Though I never had the pleasure of seeing Mr. Fry, yet from correspondence I learned what manner of man he was—how kind, upright and good; ever ready to impart his great and arduously-acquired stores of knowledge. . . .

In all his writings, too, there could be seen something far deeper than the knowledge apparent in every sentence, a reverence and love for everything good and noble, and especially for Him who is the sum and substance of that Word whose history he did so much to unravel.

I am, yours sincerely,

JOHN ANGUS.

From G. Bullen, Esq., British Museum.

15th November, 1886.

Dear Mrs. Fry,

. . . I have been exceedingly grieved to hear of the death of my old and esteemed friend, Mr. Fry. A deal of knowledge has died with him, especially in the particular branch of research to which he chiefly devoted himself—the bibliography of our English Bible. Only one man that I ever knew at all approached him in that branch of knowledge, namely, the late Henry Stevens, who had a great admiration for your husband. . . .

I remain, dear Mrs. Fry,

Yours most truly,

GEORGE BULLEN.

From the Rev. John Earle, M.A., Oxford.

23rd November, 1886.

Dear Mrs. Fry,

. . . My intercourse with him opened a new and delightful field of observation; also, it added a thread to the strength to my interest in Holy Scripture, and it has left results of knowledge and of grateful reminiscences towards him.

I am, yours sincerely,

JOHN EARLE.

From the Rev. Dr. Hooppell, M.A., LL.D., Byer's Green,
Co. Durham.

23rd November, 1886.

Dear Mr. Fry,

. . . I shall never forget the pleasant hours I spent at Cotham some few years ago, when your father showed me his unrivalled collection of biblical treasures; and I have not unfrequently since recalled the scene spread before my eyes then, when addressing meetings of the Bible Society. . . .

Very faithfully yours,

T. Fry, Esq., M.P.   R. E. Hooppell.

From Edward Arber, Esq., F.S.A., 35, Wheeley's Road,
Birmingham.

10th May, 1887.

Dear Mr. Fry,

. . . I was vexed to see the death of your dear father in the papers. He was one of the pillars of English bibliography. Our losses in that department of knowledge of late have been enormous. Francis Fry, Henry Bradshaw, Henry Stevens and Cornelius Walford all died within a short time, and I never expect to meet with their equals. I have many pleasant memories of your father, and I respected him will all my heart. He has rendered noble service in the bibliography of our printed English Scriptures, for which I hope his name will be held through many years to come in affectionate memory.

With the kindest regards, I am ever,

Most faithfully yours,

Theodore Fry, Esq., M.P.   Edward Arber.

APPENDIX B.

Cotham Tower.

From Felix Farley's " Bristol Journal," June 26th, 1779 :—

" There is now building on Cotham Hill, by Mr. Partridge, a round tower, which, if carried to about twice its present height, will be the grand landmark of the City of Bristol in distant parts, and command a prospect of Kingswood on one side, and the town and its environs on the other."

Memorandum by F. Fry.

The old windmill, mentioned in " Westbury's " interesting communication, is depicted in Millerd's bird's-eye view of " The Citty of Bristoll," published about 1672, and in Rocque's plan of Bristol, published in 1753. In the latter " Cotham's Lodge " and " The Gallows," with the paths leading from them to the mill, are clearly shown.

The lower part of the tower in the grounds of Tower-house, Cotham, the highest part of Cotham, was originally part of a windmill used for grinding snuff, as was also the old windmill since converted into the observatory on Clifton-down. The windmill at Cotham was raised many years ago to form an observatory or "look-out." My information is derived from having perused the ancient title deeds of Cotham as it is now called. The earliest deed, a very old one, describes the whole district as "Codde Downes," and mentions the windmill on the top of the Downes, and states it was in the occupation of a "tobacco spinner" (as tobacco manufacturers were then called), and used for grinding snuff.

At one time it was in the occupation of John Innys, tobacco spinner, who resided at Redland Court, and whose manufactory was on the site of the Wool-hall in Thomas-street. In later deeds Codde Downes became Codd or Cod Down, Coat Down, Coat Ham and Cod Ham, and at last Cotham, as it is now spelt.

APPENDIX C.

WHEN at Mayence a few months since, I visited
the house in which Gutenberg first exercised his
newly-discovered art of printing. The present
occupier is a wine merchant, who obligingly showed
me everything which now remains connected with
the inventor; and as it may not be known to many
that part of his first printing-press has been found

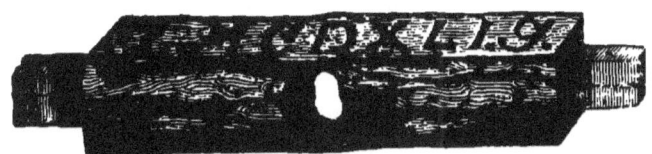

in that house, it may be interesting to give a short
account of this precious relic, and the situation in
which it has so long remained.

The house has been much altered since the time
of Gutenberg, and the level of the street has been
raised several feet, so that what is now the cellar
was then the ground floor of the building. In
1857 Mr. Borzner (the late proprietor), in excavat-
ing underneath his house, discovered the walls

E

which had formed the original cellars, and on removing some of these, he found a recess or closet, in which were the remains of the press and some other materials. I visited the place in which it was discovered. The room had evidently been whitewashed and furnished with windows. The principal piece of the press was the top cross-beam, in which worked the upright screw. It was made of oak, and provided with the necessary hole in the centre, in which the screw thread is still visible. It is about 3 feet 4 inches long, and upon one side is deeply cut the following inscription: " J. MCDXLI. G." This occupies the whole space, and there is no doubt that the unusual mode of expressing 400 by CD was adopted because there was not sufficient room for the CCCC. The J and G are the initials of the printer. The above is a representation of the relic, which is now resting on a velvet cushion in a glass case.

With it were found some other pieces of wood, supposed to have been parts of the press, a few stone mulls, used no doubt for grinding the ink, and four coins, one of each of the reigns of Augustus, Trajan, and Marcus Aurelius, and one illegible.

Gutenberg, on his return from Strasburg about the year 1445, settled in a portion of the house of his paternal uncle, John Geinsflesh, the Hotel du Jungen, where he erected his press; and from the date on the beam it must have been used in Strasburg, where Gutenberg resided in 1441, in the production of prints from wood blocks, which he is known to have executed in that town. The locality in which the discovery was made confirms the opinion generally held, that he worked in secret, in order that the invention might not become public. John Schœffer, the eldest son of Peter Schœffer, at the end of a work which he printed in 1515, after giving an account of the invention of printing, says:—"That John Fust and Peter Schœffer kept the art secret, binding with an oath all their assistants and servants on no account to reveal it, which art was afterwards spread abroad in different lands in the year 1462[*] by the same assistants."[†]

So many years having elapsed, from 1441 the

---

[*] In 1462 Mayence was taken by Adolphe of Nassau, and Fust's printing-office destroyed, and during this commotion the workmen went to Rome, Cologne, Basle, Strasburg, &c.

[†] *Breviarum Historiæ Francorum*, Mayence, 1515.

date on the press, to the year 1450, when Gutenberg began to print, without any result of his
labours being known to us, the following passage
from the *Cologne Chronicle*, printed in 1499, may,
to some extent serve as an explanation, and is
given on the authority of Zell, who is supposed to
have been one of the workmen either in the office
of Gutenberg or in that of Fust and Schœffer :—
" The most worthy art of printing was first discovered in Germany, at Mayence on the Rhine,
and was a great honour for the German nation.
This took place from 1440 to 1450, during which
time the art was perfected and what belongs to it.
But in the year which is called 1450, a golden
year (*i.e.* a jubilee year) they began to print, and
the first book printed was the Bible, and it was
printed in a thick letter, which is the letter now
printed in missal books." . . . " The first
discoverer of printing was a citizen of Mayence,
and his name was John Gutenberg." . . " The
commencement and progress of the said art was
related to me by Master Ulrich Zell, printer at
Cologne, in 1499, through whom the art was first
brought to Cologne." . . . . " There are also
fanciful people who say that books were printed

before, but this is not true, nor in no country are books to be found printed before that time."*

The discovery of the press, and the situation in which it was found, are additional proofs that Mayence was the birth-place of the art of printing, and that the honour of the invention belongs to John Geinsfleish Gutenberg.

FRANCIS FRY.

Cotham, Bristol, 1st Mo. 1861.

---

* *Cologne Chronicle*, Koelhoff, 1499, p. 311

APPENDIX D.

Some readers may be interested in knowing something about the Bibles in Mr. Fry's collection. These, with the Testaments and a few parts, number nearly 1,300. They are mostly in English, but amongst them are a considerable number in foreign languages, chiefly first editions. It would be impossible to allude to more than a few in these pages, but the following are of great interest :—

The first Bible in English, translated by Miles Coverdale. 1535.

The Reprints of the same, by Nycolson, in folio and 4to. 1537.

The three Reprints, in 4to., by Hester, Froschover and Jugge. 1550 and 1553.

The Pentateuch, by Tyndale. 1530.

Six Bibles of Tyndale's Version (including Matthew's). 1537 to 1551. Printed by John Day, Day and Seres, &c.

The Great Bible, Cromwell's Earl of Essex. 1539.

The Cranmer Bibles. Six Editions with the two variations, 1540 and 1541 (being the standard set of nine described on pages 47-50), and fifteen other Editions, by Whitchurch, Grafton, Carmarden, &c. &c. 1541 to 1569.

Four of Taverner's Version. 1539 to 1550.

Seventy-five Editions of the Genevan Version. 1560 to 1663.
    Printed at various places.
Nineteen Editions of the Bishops' Versions. 1568 to 1575.
The Bassandine (first printed in Scotland). 1579.
The Welsh Bible. 1588 to 1654.

The various Editions of the Authorised Version, amounting to several hundred, it would be impossible to specify in detail.

Amongst the New Testaments are—

Eight Editions of Coverdale's Version (two not dated). 1538 to 1549.
Twenty-eight Editions of Tyndale's Versions, all of which are described in Mr. Fry's Book referring to them.
Three Editions of Cranmer's Version. 1547 to 1548.
The first in the Welsh (1567) and Irish languages (1602).
Twenty-eight Editions of the Genevan Version. 1557 to 1586.
Eighteen Editions of the Bishops' Versions. 1581 to 1595.

The Bibles, Testaments, &c. in foreign languages number about one hundred and fifty. Amongst them, many being First Editions in their respective languages, are the—

Latin—Gunther Zainer, Augsburg	...	no date.
Eggistein (no place) ...	...	1468.
Koburger, Nuremburg ...		1475.
Peter Schoeffer, junr., Worms	...	1529.
Italian (Venice)	...	1487.
Dutch	...	1525.
,, ...	...	1568.

German (Wittenberg, Zurich, Dresden, &c.),

				1522 to 1584.
French	...	...	... 1526, 1530,	1581.
Luther's German	...	...	...	1584.
Pagnini (first in Verses)		...	...	1528.
Swedish	...	...	...	1541.
Danish	...	...	...	1550.
Spanish (Old Testament)		...	...	1553.
,,	...	...	...	1569.
Polish	...	...	...	1561.
Italian Protestant	...	...	...	1562.
Bohemian	...	...	...	1570.
Sclave	...	...	...	1581.
Icelandic	...	...	...	1584.
Romansche Engadina Bassa		...	...	1679.
Malagassy	...	...	...	1885.
German New Testament (Strasburg)			...	1525.
,,	,,	(Worms)	...	1591.
French	,,	(Antwerp)	...	1529.
Italian	,,	(Diodati)	...	1608.

Also a great many Psalters, Prophets, and
other portions of the Sacred Volume in various
languages.

APPENDIX E.

Works by the late Francis Fry, F.S.A.

THE FIRST NEW TESTAMENT

Printed in the English Language (Worms, 1525). Translated by
WILLIAM TYNDALE.
Reproduced in facsimile, with an introduction.
Printed for the Editor, 1862. 8vo. cloth, £8. A few copies on vellum
and some on large paper.
This is exact from the only copy known perfect, but without a Title,
in the Baptist College Library, Bristol.

A DESCRIPTION OF THE GREAT BIBLE, 1539,

And the Six Editions of CRANMER's Bible, 1540 and 1541 ; also of the
Five Editions, folio, of the A. V., dated 1611, 1613, 1617, 1634, 1640.
Illustrated with Titles, Passages from the Editions, the Genealogies, and
the Maps, copied in facsimile. Also with an identification of every leaf
of the Great Bible and the Six Cranmers, and of many leaves of the
other editions, on 51 plates.
Together with an ORIGINAL LEAF of each of the Editions described.
Demy Folio, on thick toned paper ; the plates on imitation old paper,
made expressly.
Price £5. Half morocco. A few copies on fine selected vellum, £20.

THE BIBLE BY COVERDALE, 1535.

Remarks on the Titles ; the Year of Publication ; the Preliminary ;
the Water-marks, &c. With facsimiles.
8vo., 10/- Large paper, 21/- A few on vellum. 1867.

A Bibliographical Description of
TYNDALE'S NEW TESTAMENTS
AND OF
TWO EDITIONS OF THE BISHOPS' VERSION.
Handsomely printed on thick toned paper, red lines on every page.
Cloth, gilt tops, £3 3s. A few on large thicker paper, £6 6s.

F

Reproductions in Facsimile, with Introductions by F. FRY.

THE PROPHETE JONAS,

With an Introduction before Teachinge to Understonde Him
By WILLIAM TYNDALE,

To which is added a facsimile of COVERDALE'S VERSION OF JONAH.
8vo. Price 10/-. On *old* paper, £1. A few copies on vellum. 1862.

This work has been so long lost that no copy was known to exist. It is not in the first or any other edition of the Bible, called Tyndale's, or any other Bible.

A PROPER DIALOGE

Betwene a Gentillman and a Husbandman, eche Complaynynge to other their Miserable Calamite through the Ambicion of Clergye with a
COMPENDIOUS OLDE TREATYSE,

Shewynge howe that we ought to have the Scripture in Englysshe printed by HANS LUFT. 1530.

8vo. Price 10/- On *old* paper, £1. A few copies on vellum. 1863.

These were written by some one who strongly advocated the *new learning*. The dialogue is in rhyme.

THE SOULDIERS POCKET BIBLE.

Printed at London by G. B. and R. W. for G. C. 1643.
Small 8vo. Price 5/- A few copies on vellum. 1862.

This was the Pocket Bible, there can be no doubt, which was supplied to Cromwell's army; only one copy known in England.

THE CHRISTIAN SOLDIERS' PENNY BIBLE.

Showing from the Holy Scriptures the Soldier's Duty and Encouragement.
London : Printed by R. SMITH for SAM. WADE, 1693.
Small 8vo. Price 5/- 1862.

This is also a rare tract. It is nearly a reprint of the Souldiers Pocket Bible.

London : H. SOTHERAN & Co., 36, Piccadilly.